JIMMY McRAY WAS DIFFERENT

© Copyright 1999 by ARO Publishing.
All rights reserved, including the right of reproduction in whole or
in part in any form. Designed and produced by ARO Publishing.
Printed in the U.S.A. P.O. Box 193 Provo, Utah 84603

ISBN 0-89868-481-1–Library Bound
ISBN 0-89868-482-X–Soft Bound
ISBN 0-89868-483-8-Trade

A PREDICTABLE WORD BOOK

JIMMY McRAY
WAS DIFFERENT

Story by Janie Spaht Gill, Ph.D.
Illustrations by Gerald Rogers

ARO PUBLISHING

Different indeed, was Jimmy McRay.

When he walked toward his classmates, they all ran away.

At recess he sat under shade trees to read.

"What a bookworm you are!" the children would tease.

The lunches he brought would make classmates scream,

like chocolate bar pizza topped with mustard greens.

9

The clothes that he wore were mismatched and loud.

All heads would turn around when he walked through a crowd.

One day he sketched out an invention to make.

"I could build that," he said, "even though I'm just eight."

So, Jimmy got busy, he worked day and night.

He measured and hammered to make it just right.

After weeks of hard work, Jimmy finished at last.

"Tomorrow, wait outside," he said to the class.

The next morning, the students stood outside, and then…

they saw something shiny, quickly rounding the bend.

19

As Jimmy screeched to a halt in his shiny go-cart,

the students all cheered, "Wow, Jimmy you're smart!"

21

This sparked fresh ideas in each student's head.

The children said, "Yes!" Then, off Jimmy sped.